JANE HISSEY

Little Bear's Dragon

and other stories

HUTCHINSON

London Sydney Auckland Johannesburg

For Elizabeth

First published in 1999

1 3 5 7 9 10 8 6 4 2

First published in the United Kingdom
in 1999 by Hutchinson Children's Books
Random House UK Limited
20 Vauxhall Bridge Road,
London SW1V 2SA

Random House Australia (Pty) Limited
20 Alfred Street, Milsons Point, Sydney
New South Wales 2061, Australia

Random House New Zealand Limited
18 Poland Road, Glenfield
Auckland 10, New Zealand

Random House South Africa (Pty) Limited
Endulini, 5A Jubilee Road, Parktown 2193, South Africa

Random House UK Limited Reg. No. 954009

A CIP catalogue record for this book is available
from the British Library

ISBN: 0 09 176882 9

Printed in Singapore

Contents

Little
Bear's Dragon

OLD Bear was reading a story to Little Bear. It was a very exciting book about a dragon who lived in a secret cave. Little Bear had to hide under a blanket every time Old Bear made the dragon roar 'Grrr ...'

'Are there any real dragons?' asked Little Bear.

'I don't think so,' said Old Bear. 'I haven't seen any myself. But we could make you a dragon mask if you like. Then you could pretend to be a real dragon and surprise the other toys.'

'Oh, yes,' squeaked Little Bear, 'and I could live in a cave and be really fierce!'

'Just like the dragon in the story,' said Old Bear. He searched through a basket of odds and ends and pulled out some small empty boxes. 'This one looks the right size for your head,' he said. 'I'll cut it in half and join the pieces together with paper fasteners. Then the dragon will have a mouth that opens and shuts.'

'And will it breathe fire?' asked Little Bear.

'I don't think I can manage *that*,' laughed Old Bear. 'Let's see what else we can find,' he added, peering into the basket.

'What about this?' cried Little Bear, pulling out an old tablecloth. 'I could make it into the dragon's cave.'

'That's a lovely idea,' said Old Bear. 'It's just the right colour.'

While Old Bear began to make the dragon

mask, Little
Bear hurried
off with the
tablecloth to
build his cave.
    First he
draped the cloth
over a chair.
Then he
arranged
the folds
in the
shape
of a
cave.

When he had finished, he scrambled out of the entrance to see what it looked like from the outside. 'It's lovely,' he cried. 'A dragon could really hide in there,' and he ran off to tell Old Bear.

When Little Bear found him, Old Bear had already cut out and painted the dragon's head.

'I like the way the mouth opens,' said Little Bear, 'but it isn't quite scary enough yet, is it?'

'No, you're right,' said Old Bear, examining the mask. 'It needs some nice sharp teeth.'

On a sheet of white paper, Little Bear drew a long row of pointy teeth – up and down, up and down. Then he cut them out with a pair of scissors.

When the teeth were finished, Old Bear stuck them inside the dragon's mouth and added a piece of ribbon to make a long forked tongue.

'*Now* it looks fierce,' said Little Bear, taking a step back. 'I'm glad I'll be inside it. I wouldn't want to see it from the outside!'

Old Bear finished making a hole in the bottom of the dragon mask. Then he lifted it up and slipped it over Little Bear's head.

'Grrr,' said Little Bear, as loud as he could.

'You look like a very fierce dragon now,' said Old Bear.

'And I even have my own cave,' said the little dragon. 'I'll show you.'

When they arrived at the mouth of the cave, Little Bear hurried inside. 'It's really nice in here,' he called. 'Come and see.'

'Not with a scary dragon like you in there,' said Old Bear. 'I'll go and see whether I can find something for your dragon's tail.'

While Old Bear was away, Little Bear practised his roars. He tried the sort of little roars that a baby dragon might make and then he tried louder ones to sound more fierce.

Soon all the roaring made him feel quite tired so he decided to lie down on the floor of the cave and see whether there was enough room for a small dragon to rest.

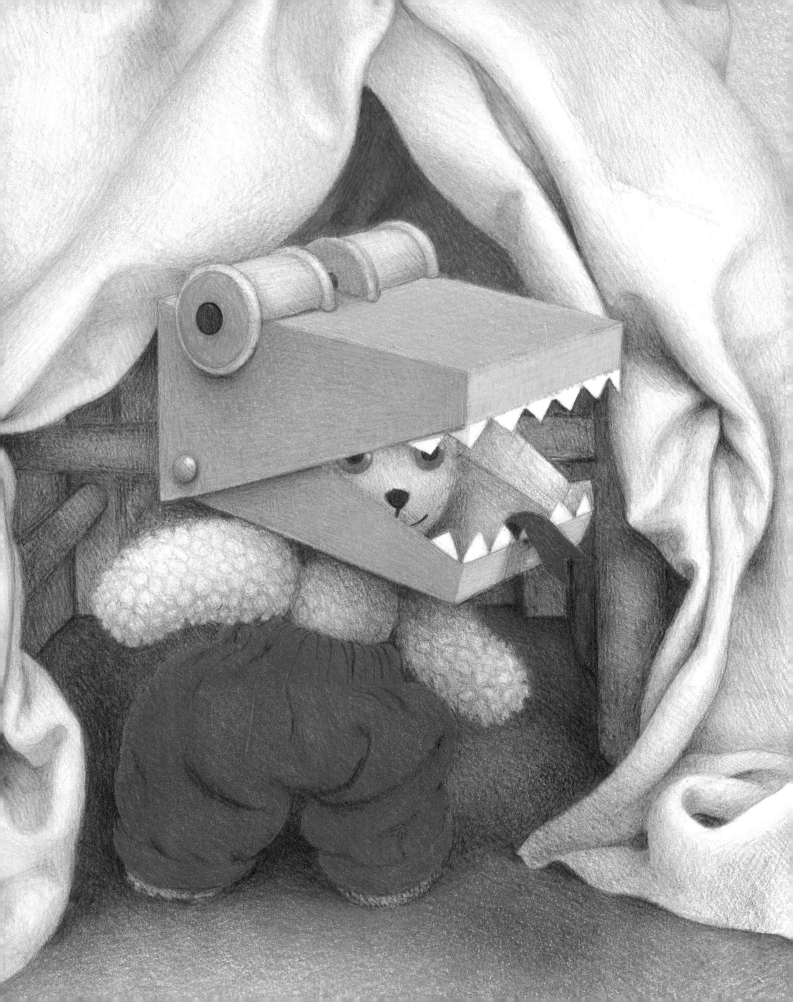

It was nice and cosy in the cave and in no time at all Little Bear had settled down in a corner and fallen fast asleep.

He was still sleeping when Jolly and Rabbit arrived. They didn't notice the dragon's cave at first.

'Can you hear a sort of breathing noise?' asked Rabbit, gazing round the room.

'It sounds like someone snoring,' said Jolly, 'but I can't see anyone.'

Suddenly Rabbit spotted Little Bear's cave. 'What's *that*?' he whispered. He tiptoed over and pressed his ear against the cloth. 'The breathing noise is coming from in here,' he said quietly. Very slowly he pulled back a corner of the tablecloth. 'Aaah!' he cried, leaping back. 'It's a dragon! Quick! Run!'

Jolly galloped towards the door and bumped straight into Sailor who was just coming into the room.

'Where are you going in such a hurry?' asked Sailor. 'We're escaping from a dragon,' panted Jolly. 'It's just over there, behind that cloth.' 'And is it breathing fire?' asked Sailor nervously.

'Not right now,' said Rabbit. 'It's asleep, but I'm sure it might do at any moment.'

'Well, I'll fetch some water to put its fire out,' said Sailor. 'Just in case.'

'Good idea,' said Rabbit. 'Dragons are probably frightened of water, but hurry, Sailor. It might wake up at any minute.'

'What *other* things are dragons frightened of?' asked Jolly.

'Only other dragons, I suppose,' said Rabbit. 'Bigger ones.'

'Perhaps we could pretend to be a bigger one?' suggested Jolly. 'We could make a sort of dragon suit and get inside it. And when the little dragon woke up, it would see the really big one and stay in its cave and not breathe fire on us.'

'It might even run away,' said Rabbit, 'and never be seen again.'

Just then Sailor
returned with two
buckets of water.

Rabbit couldn't wait
to tell him of Jolly's
plan. 'We're going
to dress up as a
big dragon,' he
said, 'and
frighten the
little dragon
away. But we
might still need
the water,' he
added, 'in
case the plan
doesn't work.'

'I'll guard the
cave if you like,' said Sailor bravely, 'while you
go and make the dragon costume.'

Jolly and Rabbit hurried
away leaving Sailor
sitting as close to the cave
as he dared, watching
the tablecloth for any
sign of movement.
Some time later, he
was still staring so
hard at the

dragon's cave that he didn't hear Old Bear come into the room.

'Hello,' called Old Bear. 'Have you seen Little Bear or is he still in the cave?'

Before Sailor could reply, there was a huge roar and into the room marched a large green dragon with a long yellow neck and sharp white teeth. Sailor nearly threw his buckets of water at it but realised just in time that it was only Jolly and Rabbit in their dragon costume.

'Quick,' he called. 'There's not a moment to lose. Old Bear says that Little Bear is in the cave. The dragon must have captured him.'

'We'll save him,' cried Jolly. 'Hurry, Sailor, come under here with us!'

Before Old Bear could explain about Little Bear and the storybook dragon, Sailor had joined Rabbit and Jolly in the dragon costume, and the eight-legged monster rushed towards the cave, roaring and stamping its feet.

'What's all the noise?' cried the Little Bear dragon, as it staggered sleepily out of the table-cloth cave.

'Oh, no,' groaned Jolly. 'It's wearing Little Bear's trousers. It must have eaten Little Bear!'

Old Bear tried to explain. 'It's all right,' he began, but before he could say more, the big dragon roared as loud as it could.

'Help, help!' cried the little dragon, as it scrambled back into the cave.

Rabbit peeped out from under the dragon costume. 'It worked!' he cried. 'We've frightened it away.'

'But we were too late to save Little Bear,' sniffed Jolly.

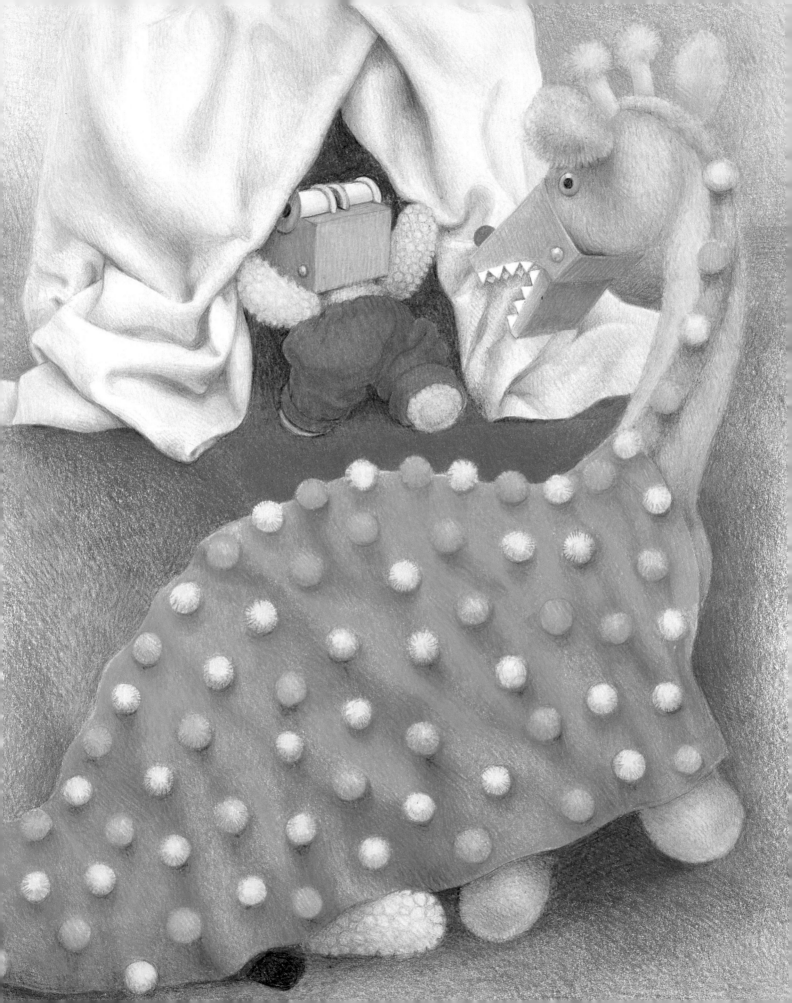

Old Bear hurried over. 'Let's see, shall we?' he said, smiling. 'I think I might have a surprise for you.'

He stood by the entrance to the cave and called, 'Come out, little dragon.'

And out it came … very slowly.

Then Old Bear took hold of the dragon's cardboard-box head and carefully lifted it off.

And there was Little Bear looking rather anxious, but all in one piece.

Old Bear picked him up and carried him over to the big dragon. 'Now don't worry,' he said. 'This isn't a real dragon either.'

'Isn't it?' said Little Bear. 'Are you sure?'

'Quite sure,' said Old Bear. 'Jolly, Rabbit and Sailor are in there.'

'Did they think I was a real dragon too?' asked Little Bear.

'They did,' laughed Old Bear, 'and they tried to frighten you away. But you are all

safe now and you
must be hot enough to
breathe fire after
wearing those dragon
costumes. Come
with me and we'll have
a nice cool drink.'
'Then will you read us
another story?'
asked Little Bear.
'About something not
quite so scary this time.'

The
Boat Race

IT was a fine, warm summer's day and Bramwell Brown and his friends were exploring the garden shed.

'There's so much to play with in here!' said Little Bear. 'I don't think we'll ever want to go back to the house.'

Bramwell had found a heap of old newspapers and was busy tearing them into sheets.

'What are you doing?' asked Little Bear.

'Well, watch carefully,' said Bramwell, 'and I'll show you.' He folded one of the pieces of paper in half and then in half again. After a few more folds he held up the finished model for Little Bear to see.

'It's a boat!' cried Little Bear, taking it from Bramwell to have a closer look. 'If we had more we could have a race with them down the stream.'

'That would be fun,' said Rabbit. 'Could you make us all one please, Bramwell?'

So Bramwell made a whole fleet of paper boats – one for each of the other toys. 'Let's try them out in Sailor's bath,' he suggested.

Sailor was having a wonderful time. He had filled an old tin bath with water from the hose and was rowing round and round in a little wooden boat. 'Ahoy there!' he called when the others popped their heads over the side. 'Are you going to join me?'

'We'd like to try one of our boats in your bath,' said Rabbit.

'Of course,' said Sailor. 'There's plenty of room.'

'Bramwell made us *all* boats,' explained Little Bear. 'We want to race them down the stream.'

'I'll see if mine floats,' said Rabbit, lowering his boat into the water and giving it a push.

The little boat sailed well at first. But then they all watched sadly as it began to go soggy and finally fell over in the water.

'Oh no!' cried Little Bear. 'It's sinking. What can we do?'

Bramwell examined his paper boat. 'Actually,' he said thoughtfully, 'I think the reason they are no good in water is that they aren't boats at all … they're hats … pirate hats.'

'But we can't have a boat race with *hats*,' muttered Duck.

'Of course we can,' said Bramwell. 'We'll wear the pirate hats and build ourselves a proper boat. One we can get inside.'

'A boat *each*,' cried Little Bear, pulling his hat over his ears.

'Well, we could build two boats,' said Bramwell, 'and Sailor could sail his own. That means we'd have three and that's enough for a race.'

Everyone thought this sounded fun and they all went back to the shed to look for boat-building materials. There were lots of bits and pieces to choose from.

Rabbit found a little wooden basket behind the door.

'This is a good boat shape,' he said, pulling it out to have a closer look. 'You and I would just fit in here, Little Bear.'

Little Bear peered into the basket. At the bottom was an old tea cloth. 'And this could be our sail,' he said. 'All we need now is a mast and we'll be ready.'

'Our boat won't need a mast,' said Bramwell. 'Jolly has a long neck and he can hold our sail.'

'What sail?' asked Duck, looking around.

Bramwell picked up an umbrella. 'I thought this might do,' he said. 'If Jolly holds it up the wind will catch it and blow us along.

'And this is going to be our boat,' called Jolly. He had found a pile of sticks and, with Sailor's help, was tying them together side by side. 'It's a sort of raft,' said Jolly proudly. 'It'll be very strong when it's finished.'

'It'll need to be,' muttered Duck, 'if we're

all going to float on it. I don't want to get my feet wet.'

Very soon all three boats were ready and

waiting by the door of the shed – the raft for Jolly, Duck and Bramwell, the basket boat for Rabbit and Little Bear, and Sailor's yacht.

The toys started to pull the boats out of the shed and down the path to the stream.

When nobody was looking, Sailor tied his boat to Bramwell's and had a ride all the way to the water.

'Hats on!' cried Bramwell when they were standing on the bank of the stream.

'I haven't got a pirate hat,' said Rabbit. 'Don't you remember? Mine sank when it was trying to be a boat.'

'Never mind, Rabbit,' said Little Bear. 'You can borrow mine when we're afloat. Can you give the boat a push, please?'

Rabbit pushed the boat as hard as he could. He was just about to jump in when a big gust of wind filled the tea cloth sail and Little Bear set off down the stream.

'Wait for me!' cried Rabbit, running along the bank.

The same gust of wind had caught Jolly's umbrella and the raft didn't even need a push. It sailed off from the bank with Bramwell, Duck and Jolly on board – and Sailor, whose boat was still tied to the raft, trailing along behind.

Rabbit was still running along beside Little Bear's boat. 'You're going too fast,' he puffed. 'Lower the sail and you'll slow down.'

Little Bear pulled. 'It's stuck,' he shouted. 'I'll climb up the mast and unhook it.' Little Bear began to scramble up the mast. He was so busy climbing that he didn't notice the bridge across the stream.

'Oh no, look out!' cried Rabbit, but he was too late. The mast struck the bridge and the boat fell over in the water.

Little Bear flew from the top of the mast, bounced off Jolly's umbrella and landed in Bramwell's outstretched paws. 'Phew! That was lucky,' gasped Little Bear, as Bramwell set him down on the deck of the raft.

'Not for us,' moaned Duck, looking at the water around his feet. 'This raft was only meant for three and there are four of us on here now.'

They floated under the bridge, but the raft was getting lower and lower in the water.

'HELP!' shouted Little Bear. 'We're going to sink! Where's Rabbit? He was there on the bank a minute ago.'

'HELP!' shouted Bramwell, Jolly and Duck together.

And then they heard a familiar sound. Looking up they saw the little wooden aeroplane, with Rabbit as pilot, flying across the garden towards them.

'Hurray!' they cried. 'Rabbit is coming to save us!'

The plane flew round in a big circle, then low down over the stream.

'Catch this,' shouted Rabbit, throwing down the end of a long rope. 'I'll tow you to the bank.'

Bramwell just grabbed the rope before it slipped into the water. He tied it securely to the front of the raft just as Sailor managed to untie his boat from the back. Rabbit held tightly to the other end of the rope and began to pull the sinking raft slowly towards the bank while the little yacht with Sailor on board sailed on down the stream.

When everyone was safe on dry land, Rabbit dropped his end of the rope, flew round in a circle and landed the little plane on the grass. He climbed down and bounded over to where the others were waiting.

'Oh Rabbit! You were *wonderful!*' cried Little Bear.

'You rescued us just in time,' said Jolly, in a slightly wobbly voice.

'It's a pity that nobody won the race,' muttered Duck.

But as they spoke Sailor came rowing his boat back up the stream. '*I* must have won the race,' he called. 'I'm the only one left with a boat!'

'Well done, Sailor,' said Jolly. 'In future, I think we'll leave all the sailing to you!'

'And I shall make Rabbit a new hat,' laughed
Bramwell, 'but instead of a pirate's hat, I think
it should be a pilot's hat, don't you?'

The
Three Bears

IT was a warm summer's day and all the toys were sitting under a tree in the garden. They were watching Bramwell and Jolly trying to make an old curtain into a hammock and waiting for Old Bear to tell them a story.

'Now this is a story about Goldilocks and the three bears,' began Old Bear.

'Who's Goldilocks?' asked Little Bear.

'She's a little girl,' said Old Bear, sighing. Little Bear already knew who Goldilocks was because he'd heard the story so many times before.

'The three bears lived in a cottage in the middle of a wood — ' Old Bear continued.

'I like this story,' interrupted Little Bear. 'Especially the bit about the porridge.'

'We'll never get to that bit, if you don't listen,' laughed Old Bear. 'Now one day Goldilocks was walking in the wood when she came to a little house — '

'Can I have some porridge?' asked Little Bear.

'You don't need porridge on a hot, sunny day,' said Duck. 'Porridge is to warm you up.'

Little Bear shivered. 'I am feeling a bit chilly,' he said. 'Just here,' he went on, rubbing his tummy.

Bramwell Brown smiled. 'Well, I was going to get something to eat soon. So perhaps we could have some porridge for lunch.'

'Can I help?' asked Little Bear.

'No, you stay here and listen to the rest of the story,' said Bramwell. 'I won't be long.'

The toys settled down again as Old Bear told them about Goldilocks arriving at the house of the three bears. They had just reached the end of the story when Bramwell returned. He was carrying a tray laden with a steaming dish of porridge and a pile of bowls and spoons.

'Come and have some porridge!' he called to Jolly who was still struggling with the hammock.

'I want to get this up first,' replied Jolly. 'I've only fixed one side to the trees.'

'It looks just like a theatre curtain hanging like that,' said Bramwell.

'So it does,' said Old Bear, looking thoughtful. 'Perhaps we could put on a play.'

'What's a play?' asked Little Bear.

'A sort of moving story,' said Old Bear. 'Some people pretend to do things that are in a story and the others watch them.'

'Ooh!' said Little Bear. 'That sounds fun. Can I be in the play?'

'Only if it's about someone very small,' muttered Duck.

'Why don't we do the story Old Bear has just been telling us?' said Rabbit. 'That has a baby bear in it.'

'And the bears all eat porridge,' said Little Bear.

'Actually they don't,' said Duck. 'They go out to leave it to cool down. They only eat a little bit … and the baby bear doesn't get any at all.'

'I'm not being a bear who has no food!' said Little Bear.

'Well, you could have some before we start the play,' said Bramwell, spooning some porridge into a bowl and passing it to Little Bear.

While Little Bear ate his porridge, the others went off to the shed to look for the things they would need for the play. Bramwell found two very big boxes to use for the three bears' house, and there were some middle-sized ones for making the beds and a table, and small ones for making chairs.

'We'll cut a hole in this box for the front door,' said Old Bear.

'And a hole here, for the bedroom door,' added Rabbit.

Zebra and Duck collected odds and ends that might be useful in the play and piled them into the boxes while Ruff bounced back from the house with scissors and string.

When they were ready they dragged the pile of boxes back across the garden to where the curtain hung between the trees.

'We'll make the furniture now,' said Old Bear. 'If we cut the sides off these shoe boxes, they'll make lovely little beds.'

'Who are going to be the mummy and daddy bears?' asked Little Bear.

'I'll be Daddy Bear,' said Old Bear, trying out one of the shoe-box beds. 'And perhaps Bramwell would like to be Mummy Bear! He could wear a long apron.'

Bramwell found a piece of flowery material.

He cut a hole for his head and two strips to tie the apron round his middle. 'This looks just right,' he said, as Rabbit tied a bow for him behind his back.

'Lovely,' said Old Bear. 'Now, how can we make Little Bear look like a baby?'

'Well, as he's got porridge down his front already,' said Bramwell, 'perhaps a bib would be a good idea.'

'I don't need a bib,' protested Little Bear.

'It's just for the play,' said Old Bear. 'You can take it off at the end.'

Bramwell made Little Bear a tiny white bib and tied it round his neck. 'There!' he said.

'Now that you have a costume you look like a real actor.'

'We're nearly ready to start,' said Jolly.

'But we haven't got a Goldilocks yet!' said Duck. 'She has to eat the porridge and break a chair.'

'I'll be Goldilocks,' said Little Bear.

'You can't be Goldilocks *and* Baby Bear,' said Rabbit. 'I'll be Goldilocks. I haven't had any porridge yet.'

'Goldilocks has long, golden hair,' said Duck. 'Yours is too short.'

'Well, I'll make some then,' said Rabbit, rummaging about in the odds-and-ends box. He pulled out a yellow curtain fringe and draped it over his head. 'How's that?' he said.

'Perfect,' said Old Bear. 'Now all we need is an audience. Ruff, would you go and tell every-one we're ready to begin?'

Ruff bounced off and soon returned with all

the toys. Once they had settled themselves on the blanket, Jolly grabbed the edge of the curtain and galloped across to pull it back. And there, behind the curtain, were the three bears sitting at the table ready to eat their porridge.

'This porridge is getting cold,' said Little Bear, tasting his first spoonful.

'Sshh!' said Bramwell. 'Pretend it's too hot. We're supposed to leave it to cool down.'

Little Bear blew hard on his bowl. 'This porridge is burning hot,' he said. 'Let's go for a walk while it gets colder.'

The three bears went out for a walk and almost immediately there was a rat-a-tat-tat on the front door. In fact, it was such a hard rat-a-tat-tat that the door swung open and left Rabbit standing in the doorway wearing his curtain-fringe hair.

'Is there anybody there?' he called in his Goldilocks voice. But as the door was open, he could see there was nobody in so he bounded into the room, tripped over Daddy Bear's chair, and landed head-first in the biggest bowl of porridge.

'Help!' he cried, scraping the contents of the bowl off his fur and the chair. 'This porridge is too sticky.'

He jumped on to the medium-sized chair, to try Mummy Bear's bowl. 'And this porridge is too lumpy,' he said, as he dangled his curtain fringe in it by mistake.

Finally, he took a flying leap on to Little Bear's tiny chair and squashed it completely flat.

'Whoops!' he said. 'Now I'll have to stand up to eat the rest of the porridge.'

After Rabbit had eaten
up every bit of Little
Bear's porridge, he
yawned. 'I think I'm
ready for bed now,'
he said, pushing
open the door
between the
kitchen box and
the bedroom box.

As soon as he'd
gone through the door,
the three bears came back.

'Who's been tripping over
my chair and spilling my
porridge?' said Old Bear.

'And who's been sitting on
my chair and dropping
things in my porridge?'
said Bramwell, pulling a

long piece of curtain fringe out of his bowl.

'And who has completely squashed my chair and eaten my porridge all up?' cried Little Bear.

'Never mind about the porridge,' said Old Bear. 'It's time we went for a sleep.'

'But we haven't even had our breakfast yet!' said Little Bear.

It was Old Bear who reached his bed first. 'Who's been getting porridge all over my bed?' he said.

'And who's been muddling up my bed?' said Bramwell.

'And who's bouncing up and down on my bed?' cried Little Bear. 'Why don't you lie down, Rabbit? You're meant to be Goldilocks asleep.'

'But all that porridge has made me really bouncy,' protested Rabbit. 'I don't feel tired now.'

'Well, now you're supposed to be frightened of the three bears and run away,' said Old Bear.

'Oh, I can do that,' said Rabbit. He waved his arms about and tried to look frightened. Then with an extra big bounce, he jumped straight through the open window and landed on the grass.

The audience clapped and cheered.

'Wonderful,' called Ruff, as the three bears came to the front of the box to bow. Rabbit came back through the door to join them, and when they'd finished bowing Jolly marched across with the curtain.

'That was very good,' Jolly said, popping his head round the curtain. 'Do you think I could have my porridge now?'

Bramwell looked in the saucepan. 'I'd better go and make some more,' he said. 'Little Bear has eaten most of this.'

'Well, I don't feel hungry any more,' said Little Bear, yawning. 'All that acting has made me quite tired.' He climbed into Baby Bear's shoe-box bed and snuggled down. 'Can we have another story?' he asked Old Bear sleepily.

'Well, just a quick one,' said Old Bear. 'Then we'd better put everything away.'

Old Bear sat down on the grass. 'Once upon a time …' he began, but when he looked down, the baby bear was already fast asleep.

The Birthday Camp

IT was Little Bear's birthday and the toys were all lying around, full of birthday cake and resting after a long game of musical cushions.

'That was a lovely birthday tea,' said Little Bear. 'But what can we do now?'

'It's time to give you your birthday present,' said Old Bear. 'Bramwell has just gone to fetch it.'

Little Bear jumped to his feet. 'Oh, how exciting,' he squeaked. 'I can't wait.'

Soon, Bramwell returned pushing a basket on wheels with a big sausage-shaped parcel sticking out of the top.

'Here you are,' he said. 'Happy birthday, Little Bear!'

'Thank you very much,' cried Little Bear. 'Can I open it now, please?'

'Of course you can,' laughed Old Bear.

Bramwell lifted the parcel out of the basket and placed it on the floor.

'It's a funny shape,' said Little Bear. 'I can't guess what's inside.'

He opened the end of the parcel and pulled out something long and thin.

'It's a stick,' he said.

'There's more,' said Zebra.

Little Bear reached into the parcel and pulled out another stick. 'Two sticks,' he said.

'I'll give you a clue,' said Old Bear. 'They fit together.'

Little Bear pushed one stick on to the other. 'Oh, it's a fishing-rod,' he cried. 'And this must be the fishing-line,' he added, finding the end of a long piece of string. 'I think I've caught something already,' he laughed, as he gave the string a sharp tug.

As he pulled, everything else in the parcel slipped out at Little Bear's feet. 'Oh, what *is* it?' he cried.

'Haven't you guessed yet?' laughed Old Bear. 'It's a tent.'

Little Bear jumped up and down with excitement. 'A *real* tent! For *me*?'

'Of course it's for you,' said Duck. 'It's your birthday present.'

'But I've always wanted a tent,' cried Little Bear.

'That's what we thought,' said Old Bear.

'But why has it got fishing-rods with it?' asked Little Bear.

'Those aren't fishing-rods,' laughed Old Bear. 'They're tent poles.'

'Can I camp in the garden tonight, please?' begged Little Bear.

'Not on your own,' said Old Bear.

'I'll go with him,' said Rabbit. 'I've never been camping. It would be really fun.'

'Oh, please, Old Bear!' cried Little Bear. 'Let us sleep in the tent. It *is* my birthday.'

'Well, all right,' sighed Old Bear. 'But I'll come and help you put up the tent. It isn't easy the first time.'

'Can we go now?' asked Little Bear.

'I think you'll need to pack a few other things first,' said Bramwell. 'Let's go and see what we can find.'

Soon everyone was helping to prepare for the birthday camp. Little Bear fetched his pyjamas while Bramwell and Duck packed a parcel of left-over party food for the campers. Rabbit made sleeping bags out of two small eiderdowns by sewing them down the side and along the bottom. And Old Bear found two rucksacks and helped Little Bear and Rabbit pack everything inside.

When they were ready, Bramwell handed Little Bear a torch. 'I think you'll need this,' he said. 'It's very dark outside at night.'

Little Bear thanked Bramwell and pushed the torch inside his rolled-up sleeping bag. Then Rabbit helped him to slip his paws through the rucksack straps. But when he let go, Little Bear promptly fell over backwards.

'It's a bit *heavy*,' he said, struggling to stand up. 'I'll have to take a few things out.'

A little later, with Little Bear's rucksack much lighter, the two campers were ready to go. 'Good night, everyone,' called Little Bear. 'We'll see you in the morning.'

When they arrived in the garden, Old Bear found a nice smooth area of the lawn. 'This will be a good place for the tent,' he said, unrolling it on the grass. 'There are no lumps or bumps.'

'I'll put the poles together,' said Little Bear. 'I think I know how they go now.'

When the poles were ready, Old Bear poked them through the holes in the top of the tent

and lifted it up. Then Rabbit pushed the metal tent pegs into the ground, and Little Bear hammered them down with a mallet.

Finally Old Bear tightened the ropes that held the tent up. 'There you are,' he said, 'I don't think *that* will fall down in the night.'

'It's lovely,' cried Little Bear, unrolling his sleeping bag and pushing it into the tent. 'I want to go to bed right now.'

'I think you ought to get into your pyjamas first,' laughed Old Bear. 'Now I'm going back to the house so I'll say good night. See you in the morning. Sleep well.'

As soon as Old Bear had gone, Rabbit and Little Bear changed into their night clothes and climbed into their sleeping bags.

'Oh dear,' said Rabbit, 'I think we forgot to bring the things in from outside.'

'Don't worry,' said Little Bear. 'I'll get them.' Still in his sleeping bag, he slithered out of the tent, stood up, and jumped across the grass. 'It's like a sack race,' he laughed, as he bounced round the tent.

Suddenly the end of his sleeping bag caught one of the tent pegs. The peg flew through the air and the tent collapsed – right on top of Rabbit.

'Help!' cried Rabbit.

'It's all right,' called Little Bear. 'I'll get

you out. Where's the way in?'

'I don't know,' came the muffled reply. 'Can you pull the poles back up?' Little Bear struggled to find the rope. He gave it a big pull and slowly the heap of cloth and poles became tent-shaped again. 'Phew,' said Rabbit, poking his head out. 'That's better.' Little Bear hammered the tent peg into the ground. 'I can hardly see what I'm doing now,' he called. 'It must be nearly night-time.' He wriggled back into the tent next to Rabbit. 'This is cosy,' he said. 'Shall we go to sleep now?'

'I think we should,' said Rabbit. 'Good night, Little Bear.'

'Good night, Rabbit.'

There was silence for a moment or two. Then … 'Rabbit?' said Little Bear.

'Mmm,' said Rabbit.

'I'm a bit hungry,' said Little Bear.

'So am I!' said Rabbit. 'Bramwell packed us some of the party food, but I don't know where we left it and it's dark now. Do you know where the torch is?'

'Umm, I don't think we've got one,' said Little Bear sadly. 'I took it out to make my rucksack lighter.'

'Well, we'll just have to use the light from the

stars then,' said Rabbit, peeping outside.

Little Bear joined him and they both stared up at the night sky.

'They're quite bright, aren't they?' said Little Bear.

'That one is,' said Rabbit, pointing. 'And it seems to be getting brighter.'

'And bigger and bigger,' said Little Bear. 'Help,' he cried. 'It's going to fall on us!'

Suddenly the bright light landed right in front of them and they saw that it wasn't a star after all.

'Yoo hoo!' came a familiar voice. 'Happy Birthday, Little Bear.'

'It's Hoot!' cried Little Bear. 'We thought you were a star. Why are you carrying a light?'

'It's a lantern,' explained Hoot. 'And it's your birthday present from me. I thought it might be useful as you're camping.'

'Oh, it will be!' cried Little Bear. 'Thank you, Hoot. You see, we've put our food somewhere and we haven't got a torch to help us find it.'

'Then it's lucky I dropped in,' laughed Hoot. 'I've something else for you too,' she added, pulling out a tiny bundle and placing it in front of Little Bear.

Little Bear carefully untied the parcel and there was the smallest birthday cake he had ever seen. 'It's lovely,' he cried. 'It's just my size.'

'Well, I'm afraid I missed your birthday party because I was asleep,' said Hoot. 'So I thought we'd have another little party tonight.'

'And I can see Bramwell's food parcel now,' said Rabbit. 'In the light from the lantern.'

The toys opened the packet and tucked into the delicious left-over party food. And when they'd eaten it all, they finished the feast with pieces of the tiny birthday cake.

'Well, I thought this birthday couldn't get any better,' said Little Bear. 'But it just goes on and on. When will it *ever* end?' he added happily.

'In a few minutes, I think,' said Hoot. 'It's long past your bedtime and you must be very tired. Now you get back in your sleeping bags and snuggle down.'

'We will,' said Little Bear, yawning. 'Good night, Hoot,' and he followed Rabbit back into the tent.

Hoot stayed nearby and very soon by the light of the lantern she could see that the two tired campers were fast asleep.